How to Be Cool
in the Third Grade

How to Be Cool in the Third Grade

BY BETSY DUFFEY
Illustrated by Janet Wilson

A TRUMPET CLUB SPECIAL EDITION

Published by The Trumpet Club, Inc.,
a subsidiary of Bantam Doubleday Dell Publishing Group, Inc.,
1540 Broadway, New York, New York 10036.
"A Trumpet Club Special Edition" with the portrayal of a trumpet and two circles
is a registered trademark of Bantam Doubleday Dell Publishing Group, Inc.

Text copyright © Betsy Duffey, 1993
Illustrations copyright © Janet Wilson, 1993

ISBN 0-440-83095-8

This edition published by arrangement with Viking Penguin,
a division of Penguin Books USA Inc.

Set in 14 pt. Plantin
Printed in the United States of America
October 1994
3 5 7 9 10 8 6 4
CWO

For Bill

CONTENTS

BECOMING COOL

What is cool in the third grade? Robbie York punched his pillow and turned it over. He leaned back and closed his eyes but he could not get to sleep.

The question floated around in his head. It was a question that he had to answer before morning. He flipped his pillow over and punched it again.

Tomorrow was the first day of school. Tomorrow he would start third grade.

Something about the first day of a new school year makes everything seem bright and wonderful. New clothes. New shoes. Long sharp pencils with unchewed erasers. Sheets of fresh blank notebook paper.

Robbie thought of the new year as a chalkboard wiped clean and black, waiting for him to write on it. This year anything was possible. Anything was possible, that is, if he knew the answer to the question:

What is cool in the third grade?

If only he knew the answer, then this year everything would be perfect.

He sat up. It was useless even trying to get to sleep. He flipped on the light beside his bed.

At the foot of his bed he could see his things laid out for school. His clothes. His shoes. His new backpack.

He frowned.

The backpack was dark blue and said ROBBIE on the back in big white letters. His mother had ordered it from a catalogue.

Robbie had been afraid that she would get him one with a Smurf or a Muppet Baby on it. It was a nice plain blue one, but . . .

He reached down and picked it up. He looked at the letters on it.

ROBBIE.

He sighed.

That was one thing that he knew was not cool. A third grader should not have a baby name. He did not know a single grown-up named Robbie.

ROBERT HAYES YORK.

His real name was great. Couldn't he have just as easily been called *Robert* or *Rob*? He held his fingers over the last three letters.

ROB.

That looked so much better.

He buried his nose into the stiff canvas and smelled the newness of the material.

He unzipped it and pulled out a new spiral notebook. He opened it. The pages were clean and white.

What is cool in the third grade?

He needed a plan. A plan to become cool.

"Robbie! Robbie!"

His mother called from downstairs.

ROBBIE!

That was it! He knew what the first step to becoming cool would be . . .

Get rid of the name *Robbie*!

"Lights out now. School tomorrow."

"Okay, Mom," he called out. He took out a pencil. He didn't have much time. He didn't know the entire answer to his question, but he knew part of it. He had to have a plan. He would make a list. Quickly he wrote: HOW TO BE COOL IN THE THIRD GRADE.

Then without stopping he wrote:

1. GET RID OF THE NAME *ROBBIE*.

He smiled. Seeing his first step to becoming cool gave him a feeling of power. He felt that by writing it down he had accomplished it.

Robbie closed his notebook and put it into his backpack. He turned off his lamp and lay back in bed. He didn't feel so restless now.

He was one step closer to being cool!

It was going to be a great year.

GET JEANS

"Robbie. Robbie, time to get up!"

Robbie pulled his blanket up around his shoulders and started to turn over.

"Robbie! School today!"

SCHOOL!

It all came back to him. Today was the first day of third grade. In one motion Robbie was on his feet. This morning he was charged with a new energy. This was the year that he would be cool.

He looked at the foot of his bed, where his things were laid out for him. His backpack was still there.

It was full.

He and his best friend Doug had spent a long time yesterday carefully making out lists of supplies that they would need for third grade. Robbie's mother had taken the list to Harkin's Department Store and had bought all his supplies for him. She had put the things into the backpack for him.

Now Robbie picked up the backpack. He felt like he had better check everything himself. He unzipped the zipper and emptied it out. One by one he began to check off everything on the list.

> Pencil Box . . . . ✔
> Glue Stick . . . . ✔
> Crayons . . . . ✔
> Spiral Notebook . . . . ✔
> Number 2 Pencils . . ✔
> Ruler . . . . *Oh, no!*

He dropped the ruler as if it had burned him.

A Pretty Pony ruler!

His mother had bought him a Pretty Pony ruler.

He definitely could not show up at school with a Pretty Pony ruler.

Third graders did not have designs on their rulers. And third grade *boys* did not have Pretty Pony on anything!

His mother just didn't understand some things.

He took the Pretty Pony ruler and stuck it under his mattress. It would be better to show up without a ruler.

He leaned back and took a deep breath. How close he had come to being uncool on the first day!

"Robbie! Are you getting dressed?"

Beside the backpack were his clothes. Shorts, shirt, socks, and shoes—but different from the shorts, T-shirt, socks, and shoes that he had worn yesterday. These were his *school* clothes. His parents always said that *school* clothes should be different from *play* clothes.

Robbie picked up the shorts and frowned. They were tan and stiff and had a red belt.

The white socks were really white and did

not have colored stripes at the top like his play socks.

The shoes were brown leather lace-ups and the shirt had a collar. That was another one of his parents' rules—NO SHIRTS WITHOUT COLLARS ALLOWED AT SCHOOL. His parents had a lot of rules.

He put the shorts on. They felt scratchy.

He would have to do something about his clothes. They were not cool.

He wished that someone would tell his mother and father that third grade boys wear T-shirts *with no collars* to school and *jeans*. He was the only boy in Danville School who did not own a pair of jeans.

He began to load all the school supplies into his backpack, but when he got to the spiral notebook he stopped. He remembered his list. He had just thought of his second step to becoming cool.

He opened the notebook and wrote:

2. GET JEANS.

"Robbie! Robbie!"

His mother called from downstairs. "Breakfast in five minutes. You don't want to miss the bus, do you?"

No, he didn't want to miss the bus! Doug would be saving him a seat.

He began to hurry.

He closed his notebook and put it into his backpack. He zipped it shut and swung it onto his shoulder.

He smiled as he headed downstairs to breakfast.

Yes! It was going to be a great year!

SMILE AND SAY "CHEESE"

"There you are!" his mother called out as Robbie came into the kitchen. She was loading a roll of film into her camera.

Robbie dropped his backpack and sat down at the kitchen table. There was a big pile of pancakes on his plate. His favorite. He leaned over the plate and inhaled the aroma of the pancakes. He reached for the syrup.

His mother snapped the camera shut. She began to wind a knob on the back. His mother took pictures of everything. She had five whole scrapbooks filled with pictures of Robbie.

All the pictures were carefully labeled.

Robbie's first step.
Robbie's first toy.
Robbie's first birthday cake.
Robbie's first EVERYTHING!

Uh-oh! Today was his first day of third grade. His first time on the school bus!

She was going to take pictures at the bus stop!

NOT COOL!

He could just imagine the school bus pulling up with all the kids looking out their windows. There he would be with his mother, having his picture taken like a baby.

His mother couldn't do that to him . . . could she?

"Robbie, I thought I would walk up to the bus stop with you and take a few pictures."

She could!

Robbie stared at his pancakes. He wasn't hungry anymore. He was a third grader now. He wanted to go up to the bus stop by himself. He did NOT want to get his picture taken in front of a busload of kids.

And she would probably *kiss* him right

there on the street in front of the whole world.

He looked at her again. She had on her brightest red lipstick.

Smack!

He could just imagine it!

He tried to think of the right words to say. The words would not come.

"Oh, Robbie," she continued. "Your father and I are so proud of you. Starting third grade. Riding the school bus . . ."

She looked like she was about to CRY!

He couldn't tell her now!

Maybe his dad could help. He looked across the table at his father.

Nope. His dad had that "our baby's growing up" look, too. It was hopeless.

Smile and say "cheese," thought Robbie. Being cool was going to be harder than he thought. He picked up his fork and began to pick at the pancakes.

As he ate he watched his mother get the camera ready. Three different lenses, two filters—

"Have you seen the tripod?"

If only he could get to the bus stop without his mother. She walked out of the kitchen. Robbie heard her walk up the stairs. She was looking for the tripod. That should keep her busy for a while.

His father was still finishing his coffee, hidden behind the paper.

Robbie saw his chance and he took it.

" 'Bye, Dad," he called and headed for the door. His father didn't look up.

Quickly Robbie headed for the bus stop. It was only one block away. He stood on the corner and watched his driveway.

If the bus came on time he would make it. No pictures. No kisses.

Would the bus ever come? One more minute and his mother would be out with the camera.

"Come on! Come on!" he thought. "Come *onnnnnn!*"

He hoped that the bus wouldn't be late.

He closed his eyes. "Come *onnn!*"

Robbie heard the bus before he saw it. It came into view around the corner of Cherrywood and Franklin.

I made it! thought Robbie. *I made it.*

No camera.

No pictures.

No ki—

"Robbie! Robbie!" He saw his mother hurrying down the driveway. A large camera bag hung from her shoulder.

He had not made it.

"Oh, Robbie, I was afraid I was going to miss it."

His mother had the camera in her hand. Worse than that, she had just put on more lipstick—bright red.

He could imagine the print of the lipstick on his cheek.

Kissed by your mom in front of a busload of kids! What an uncool way to start third grade.

The bus groaned to a stop. The driver pulled on a metal bar and the door swung open.

Robbie's mother began snapping pictures. "Turn your head a little this way," she said.

Robbie ducked as he headed toward the stairs of the bus.

His mom smiled.

" 'Bye, Robbie!" she said. "Have a great day!"

The red lips came forward.

He ducked even lower.

Smack!

Direct hit! His mother had perfect aim. She got him right on the side of the face.

He thought he heard a few giggles from inside the bus.

His face felt hot.

As he hurried up the steps, he heard the camera still clicking. Then, like a sigh of relief, the door hissed and eased shut.

At least the pictures and the kisses were behind him now. In his mind he added another step to being cool to his list.

3. NO MORE KISSES AT THE BUS STOP.

He wiped his cheek with the back of his hand and started down the aisle.

He could see Doug waving at him from the back of the bus. He moved toward Doug. His first day of third grade was about to begin.

Starting now, it was going to be a great year!

BO HANEY

Halfway down the aisle Robbie could see Bo Haney.

Bo Haney was a third grader like Robbie. Bo Haney was a big third grader. Robbie's mother would probably say "big for his age."

To Robbie, Bo was big for any age. He had been in the third grade for a long, long time.

Bo was the meanest kid in the third grade, or maybe even in the whole school. Everyone knew about Bo.

Once he unraveled the back of Sarah Jane Manila's new sweater. She had to wear her winter coat for the rest of the day.

18

Once he tied Bradley Dugan's shoelaces together—around a pole. A pole in the bathroom. The *girls'* bathroom.

Once during Pet Week he fed John Bennent's pet cricket to Tom Ballan's pet frog. Then he fed Tom Ballan's pet frog to Sally Long's cat. Then he tried to feed Sally's cat to Harvey Jones's beagle, but there was a terrible fight and everyone got to go to recess early. Danville School had not celebrated Pet Week since.

Everyone knew about Bo Haney and everyone tried to stay away from Bo Haney. Robbie had spent his first three years at Danville School carefully avoiding Bo.

Slowly Robbie continued down the aisle. Before he could get all the way to the back of the bus the bus lurched forward.

Then it happened.

Later, Robbie could not tell exactly *what* had happened. All he knew was, one second he was standing, and the next second he was sitting.

The problem was that he was not sitting in an empty seat. The problem was that he was sitting in Bo Haney's seat. Worse than that, he was sitting on Bo Haney's lap.

The entire bus was silent for a second. Then Bo's voice broke the silence.

"Hey, Wobbie," said Bo, "Hey, Baby Wobbie!"

He pushed Robbie down to the floor. Robbie was so surprised that he sat on the floor and could not say a word.

"This seat is taken!"

Then Robbie got up and stumbled backward, trying to get his balance.

He tried to think of something to say. He couldn't think of a single word. With his mouth wide open, he stood looking at Bo.

"Heh, heh, heh," Bo laughed. "Can't you talk, Baby Wobbie? Can't the widdle baby say 'goo goo'?"

Bo turned around and looked at the other kids on the bus. A few of them laughed with Bo.

"Don't let it happen again, Wobbie."

Somehow Robbie's legs began to move. He

passed the other seats of the bus without looking up.

He got back to the empty seat that Doug had saved for him and sank down into it.

"Man, what did you do that for?" Doug asked. "Don't you know who that is?"

Robbie nodded. "I didn't mean to," he said. "It just kind of happened."

"Don't let that kind of thing happen again," said Doug. "It could be dangerous. Real dangerous."

"I know," said Robbie.

For a long time Robbie stared at the back of Bo's head. The fun was gone from the day. The new year was already tarnished.

If only he had said something cool to Bo. Something that would be funny and make the kids laugh, but not at Robbie.

He sighed. It was too late.

He closed his eyes and imagined what the morning would have been like if he had been cool. He saw himself in jeans walking confidently up the steps of the bus, no cameras clicking or lips smacking, the other kids calling, "Hey, Rob!" Everything would have been perfect.

He thought of his list. There seemed to be a big difference now between writing something down and actually doing it.

He slumped lower in his seat.

It might not be a great year after all.

ONE BAD APPLE

"Wait!" Robbie held up his hand to hold Doug back. They watched from the back window of the bus until Bo went inside the school building.

"Okay," said Robbie. "Coast clear."

Robbie and Doug hurried down the steps of the bus and into the building.

"Don't get Bo mad at you again," said Doug. "Whatever you do, stay away from him."

"I will," said Robbie, "believe me, I will."

Robbie looked both ways down the hall. No sign of Bo. Maybe it would be easy to avoid him.

"Come on," he said to Doug. They hurried to the third grade rooms. They would look at the names beside the doors to see which teacher they got this year.

Robbie hoped that he would get Ms. Williams. She was the nicest teacher in the third grade. She had a popcorn party in her room every Friday and she never gave homework.

They stopped in front of Ms. Williams's door first and looked at the names printed onto apples taped to the bulletin board beside the door. Doug began to call out the names of the kids who would be in Ms. Williams's class.

"Sue Adams."

"LaTisha Baker."

"Doug Daniels! I got her!" said Doug, pointing to his name on an apple. "I got her!"

Robbie crossed his fingers for luck and looked at the rest of the apples.

Please let me get Ms. Williams, he prayed silently as he scanned the apples. "Please let me get Ms. Williams."

"Here's Matt Jones," said Doug, reading off the names. "And Pat Gatrell and Bo Haney."

BO HANEY!

Doug and Robbie exchanged looks. Uh-oh!

Bo had gotten Ms. Williams. Now Robbie DIDN'T want to get Ms. Williams. He didn't want to be anywhere near Bo Haney this year.

His prayer changed. Now he didn't want to see his name on an apple.

Please DON'T let me get Ms. Williams. Please DON'T let me get Ms. Williams. Please . . .

"Justin Lewis."

"Scott Nelson."

"Robbie York!" Doug yelled. "Right here!" He pointed to an apple in the corner of the bulletin board.

"You got her, too!" said Doug. "Come on! Let's get seats together."

"Bo's in there," said Robbie. "I don't want to go in."

"Aw," said Doug. "He's already forgotten about the bus. He won't even remember you."

Robbie swallowed.

"I hope you're right," he said. Slowly he followed Doug through the door of the classroom.

"Hey, it's Wobbie!" shouted a familiar voice as Robbie made his way back to an empty seat. Bo had not forgotten.

"Yoo-hoo, Wobbie!"

Robbie opened his backpack and took out his school supplies. When he came to his notebook he opened it and peeked at his list.

"*Psst!* Hey, Wobbie." He heard Bo call him but he didn't look up. Each time Bo called him Wobbie, Robbie felt a little smaller.

But what could he do about it?

Last year when Mary Jacobs said the Pledge of Allegiance during assembly her voice had been high and squeaky. Bo had called her Squeaky for the rest of the year. The worst part was that soon all the other kids called her Squeaky, too. Now she might just as well change her name to Squeaky because that's what everyone called her.

It happened to Al-Burp MacGreagor. He used to be Albert MacGreagor. And Katie Bernard. Now she was Katie Barnyard.

Last year the names had seemed funny to Robbie. Now that he was about to become

Wobbie for the rest of his life it did not seem funny at all. When Bo changed your name it stayed changed.

He took out his pencil and marked through number one on his list.

    1. GET RID OF THE NAME *ROBBIE*.

Beside it he wrote:

    1. GET RID OF THE NAME *WOBBIE*.

It was going to be harder to be cool in the third grade than he had thought.

THE UNDERWEAR PROBLEM

In Ms. Williams's class there were only twenty minutes between lunchtime and break-time. It was during that twenty-minute period that Bo Haney managed to notify the entire third grade class that Robbie York wore Super Heroes underwear.

Twenty minutes can be a wonderfully short period of time.

It is exactly the length of time it takes:

—to ride the Total Panic Roller Coaster at Wonder World (eighteen minutes to wait in line, two minutes to ride)

—to eat a vanilla-strawberry swirl frozen yogurt with crushed Butterfingers on top (Robbie's favorite)

—to have a fire drill

Twenty minutes can also be a terribly long period of time. It is exactly the length of time it takes:

—to get a cavity filled at the dentist

—to take a pop quiz in spelling

—to eat a large helping of his mother's broccoli casserole

The twenty minutes that it took Bo to notify the class that Robbie wore Super Heroes underwear was the longest twenty minutes in Robbie's life.

Bo had noticed Robbie's Super Heroes underwear in the boys' bathroom just after lunch.

"Hey, Wobbie," he had called to Robbie, "what's that on your underwear?"

Robbie was tucking in his shirt. He looked

down at his underwear with a puzzled look. He hadn't spilled anything at lunch. What could Bo be talking about?

"Nothing," he answered.

"Yes, there i-i-is!" said Bo.

Robbie didn't like the sound of Bo's voice. It had a teasing kind of sound to it.

Bo had managed to get the attention of all the other boys in the bathroom. They all stopped washing their hands and looked over at Robbie and Bo.

"Does Baby Wobbie have widdle Super Heroes on his undies?" Bo asked in a baby voice.

Two boys at the sink snickered.

Up until that afternoon, Robbie had no idea that there was anything wrong at all with Super Heroes underwear. All his underwear had pictures on it: Super Heroes, G.I. Joe, even Cartoon Pals.

His face turned red. He was suddenly glad he hadn't worn Cartoon Pals.

Robbie hurried out of the boys' bathroom, looking down at the floor. He didn't look up until he sat down in his seat in Ms. Williams's classroom. It was then that the longest twenty minutes of Robbie's life began.

Psstt!

He looked across the classroom. He could see Bo working on something at his desk.

It was quiet reading time. Bo should not have been working on anything. Robbie couldn't concentrate on his reading. He couldn't think of anything but what was on the paper that Bo was working on.

Bo began folding the sheet of paper. He folded it once, twice, three times, then dropped it over his shoulder onto Tom Ballan's desk.

Somehow Robbie knew that the note was about him. Tom unfolded the paper, then looked over at Robbie. He poked Bo in the back and laughed quietly.

Tom folded the note and passed it back over his shoulder to Sue. She passed it to Pat.

On and on the note went.

When the note was being passed down the row of desks beside Robbie he peeked over and caught a glimpse of the note.

It was even worse than he expected.

In the middle of the page Bo had drawn a picture of a boy in a cape flying through the air like one of the Super Heroes. Under the picture Bo had written, *Baby Wobbie wears Super Heroes underwear*. He had drawn an arrow from the words to the boy.

Robbie stretched his neck even farther to read the words at the bottom of the page:

IT'S A BIRD. IT'S A PLANE. IT'S SUPER WOBBIE!

Robbie slumped down lower into his seat. He wished a black hole would open up in the floor and swallow him. He had started the day with such high hopes. Now everything seemed hopeless.

He slipped his notebook out of his desk and turned to his list. He crossed out 2. GET JEANS. Beside it he wrote GET NEW UNDERWEAR.

Jeans seemed like the least important thing in the world. Now he would settle for a pair of new underwear.

The terrible year just got worse.

BOOK BUDDIES

The fun had gone out of the first day of school. Robbie couldn't remember ever feeling this low. It was almost time to ride home on the bus. School-bus rides were no longer something to look forward to, they were something to dread.

He sat at his desk wondering how to get out of the bus ride home. Another trip with Bo would be the worst thing that he could imagine.

He looked over at Bo. Bo was carving his name into his desk with a Boy Scout knife.

Robbie had the feeling that Bo had never been a Boy Scout.

Just then, like the answer to a prayer, he heard the most wonderful words of the day:

"Bo Haney! You will remain after school for detention hall!"

Ms. Williams had found the knife.

SAVED! For now.

It would be safe to ride the bus home today.

Then he heard the second most wonderful words of the day. "It's time to announce our Book Buddies for the year."

Book Buddies! Robbie had always wanted to be a Book Buddy. Book Buddies got to help other kids with their reading. It was not easy to be chosen. You had to have all A's from the year before. You had to have all S's in behavior.

Robbie hoped his name would be called. He had all A's and all S's. He could imagine himself carrying the red notebooks. Sitting out in the hall at the two desks. Holding up the flash cards. It would be . . . well . . . cool.

He would be a great Book Buddy! If only she would choose him.

"Luke Hansen," Ms. Williams read from a piece of paper.

Robbie crossed his fingers. *She could pick me,* Robbie thought. *I always get A's.*

"Marchelle Johnson."

Robbie thought back over all of his report cards. He had never received anything but an S in behavior. He never misbehaved. *It could be me,* he thought.

"Millie Bonaphel."

Please!

"Robbie York."

ROBBIE YORK!

He had been chosen. He would be a Book Buddy this year! Robbie grinned at Ms. Williams.

"*Awwww!*" The other kids sighed out their disappointment at not being chosen. The bell rang and the children hurried out the door to get to their buses.

"Book Buddies!" called Ms. Williams. "Please stay for just a moment and get your assignments." Robbie hurried up to the front of the room with Luke, Marchelle, and Millie. Now he would find out who his buddy was. The person that he would be working with this year.

The four children clustered around the desk. "Luke, you will have Brian Hicks." Luke nodded and headed out to the bus.

"Marchelle, you will have Katie Robertson." Marchelle nodded and left, too.

"Millie, you will have Barb Green." She nodded and left.

"And Robbie, you will have Clyde Elmer Haney." Robbie did not nod. Who was Clyde Elmer Haney? They didn't have anyone in their class named Clyde Elmer. Did they?

"Now, hurry," said Ms. Williams. "You don't want to miss the bus."

Robbie headed for the door. From the back of the room a voice called, " 'Bye, Wobbie."

Bo! Bo *Haney!*

Could it be true? Could Clyde Elmer *Haney* be Bo *Haney?* It must be true.

He was Book Buddies with Bo!

SMACK!

Robbie ran out to the bus and climbed up the stairs. He sat down beside Doug and slung his backpack down.

"Who's your Book Buddy?" said Doug.

Robbie didn't answer. He rested his head back and closed his eyes.

"You okay?"

He shook his head no.

"Who'd you get?" said Doug. "You didn't get a girl, did you?"

Robbie shook his head.

"Whew! You look so bad I thought maybe you got a girl."

"I got Bo."

"What?"

"Bo," he said again.

"Man!" said Doug. He covered his forehead with his hand. "This is not good."

They rode in silence.

The bus stopped at Doug's stop.

"Don't worry," Doug said as he walked toward the front of the bus. "We'll think of something."

Robbie didn't smile. "We have to," he said, "or I'm dead tomorrow."

Robbie's stop came next. He could see his mother as they pulled up to the stop. She was waiting at the bus stop to walk him home. As they pulled closer he could see that she was wearing her brightest, reddest lipstick.

His first two steps to being cool had changed. Now his third step seemed impossible, too. With a sigh he pulled out his notebook and changed his third step to being cool:

3. PUT UP WITH KISSES AT THE BUS STOP.

Smack!

She got him again.

The doors of the bus slammed shut with a bang like the end of his hopes for a great year. His mother did not seem to notice.

"How was your day?" she asked in a cheerful voice.

"Fine." It was no use worrying her.

"How do you like your class?"

"It's okay."

"Do you know anyone in your new classroom?"

Robbie thought of Bo. "Yes," he said without enthusiasm.

"Good," she said. She seemed satisfied with that. "Oh, Robbie, there's a sale at Harkin's. I thought I'd run over there this afternoon. Mrs. Hines will watch you while I'm gone. It will only be for about an hour. I need to get you a few more things for school."

Robbie's heart sank. What would she get him this time? Pretty Pony underwear?

He wanted to say the words, "Would you mind picking up a pair of jeans for me?"

Or, "Hey, while you're there would you

see if they have any white underwear on sale?"

He sighed. No matter how many ways he thought of to say the words, they wouldn't come out of his mouth.

As his mother hurried inside to get her purse, Robbie sank down onto the front steps.

Maybe Baby Wobbie was the right name for him after all. He had made up his list with such high hopes, but he hadn't done a single thing on his list. There was a big difference between making a plan and doing the plan.

He had to stop Bo. But how?

He couldn't tell his mother. He could just see what she'd do. She would get all upset, call Mr. Hardeman, call Bo's parents, call the PTA, call the police . . . It would only make things worse.

If only he could become cool before tomorrow, before he had to be Book Buddies with Bo, everything would be okay.

Coolness was like armor, protection from

harm and teasing. Coolness was the key to happiness in the third grade. Coolness was the key to *survival* in the third grade.

Time was running out and he needed to know the answer fast. How to be cool in the third grade? It seemed impossible.

WAAA!

He walked slowly toward Mrs. Hines's house. She came out the front door pushing Tobey in his stroller. His white pacifier was stuck tightly in his mouth. Robbie could see it move in and out as the baby sucked hard on it.

"Robbie," she called to him. "Come and take a walk with us."

Robbie walked across the yard and looked down at Tobey. He wanted to push the stroller. But Mrs. Hines probably would say no. Why bother to ask? She probably thought he was a baby, too.

"How was school?"

Before he could answer, she continued. "I remember how much I used to like the first day of school . . ."

Robbie walked along in silence listening to Mrs. Hines talk. It seemed so effortless. Streams of words seemed to pour right out of her mouth with no effort at all.

"*Waaaaaaa!*"

Robbie's thoughts were interrupted.

"*Waaaaa!*" Tobey wailed again.

"What's wrong with him?" Robbie looked down with concern. "Is he hurt?" He had never heard such a scream.

Mrs. Hines laughed, "Oh, no! He does that about a hundred times a day. That's just a baby's way of telling you he needs something. Oh, look." She bent down beside the stroller. "He lost his pacifier again. I spend more time putting that pacifier back into his mouth than I do anything else these days."

She picked up the pacifier. It was attached to a long ribbon. The end of the ribbon was pinned to the front of Tobey's shirt. She put the pacifier back into Tobey's mouth. The crying stopped.

"Babies can't talk like you and me," she continued. "They can't say 'I'm hungry,' or 'I'm wet,' or 'I'm tired.' But they sure can let you know when they want something."

How simple it seemed, Robbie thought, looking down at Tobey:

Waaa! and you got whatever you wanted. He wished it was that simple when you grew up.

Waaa! New jeans would appear.

Waaa! People would stop calling you names.

Waaa! Your mother would stop kissing you at the bus stop.

They started walking again. Mrs. Hines continued talking but Robbie was not listening. He was thinking about something else.

He had never said, "I want jeans," or "Don't call me names," or "Don't kiss me at the bus stop." He had just expected everyone to automatically know what he wanted. He thought of his steps to being cool. Writing things down was not enough.

"Do it!" a voice inside him said.

"Mrs. Hines!" said Robbie, "I'll be right back." He ran as hard as he could back down the street. "I've got to tell my mother something before she leaves for the store."

"Mom! Wait!" She was just getting into the car. "Wait, Mom!" He paused to catch his breath.

"What is it, Robbie?" His mother looked concerned.

"Mom, I need some jeans."

His mother looked up at him. "Do the other kids wear jeans to school?"

"Yes," he said. "All of the other kids wear jeans to school."

"Well . . ." she said. "I guess you need some jeans, too." She smiled and sat down in the front seat. "Anything else?"

ANYTHING ELSE!

Robbie couldn't believe how easy it had been. Now she was asking him what else he wanted. He thought for a second, then smiled.

"Underwear," he said. "PLAIN WHITE underwear."

"Plain white underwear," she repeated. Then she got that "my baby's growing up" look in her eyes and Robbie took off before it was too late. In another second she would be kissing him.

"Thanks, Mom," he said over his shoulder. He headed back to Mrs. Hines and Tobey. The sun was bright now and he wanted to push the stroller.

They returned from their walk just as his mother got out of the car carrying a large shopping bag.

Robbie ran to meet her and helped her carry the bag into the house. She began taking things out of the bag. New shirts, a pair of pajamas, two packages of underwear—plain white!

"You should have seen the mothers at Harkin's buying underwear!" she said. "Why, I saw three mothers from your third grade class alone!"

Robbie smiled. He must not have been the only boy with Super Heroes underwear. He looked at the pile on the table. There was something missing. There were no jeans in the pile.

His hopes had been too high. His mother must have needed more time to get used to the idea of jeans.

"Robbie, there's one more bag in the car. Would you bring it in, please?" Did he dare to hope?

Robbie ran all the way to the car. He opened the bag so fast that he tore the sides.

YES!

Three pairs of jeans fell out onto the driveway. Three perfect pairs of jeans.

Robbie hugged the jeans to his chest and smiled. He had done it! He carried the jeans up to his room and dropped them on his bed. Then he took off his shorts and tried a pair on. It was perfect. He zipped them up and did two deep knee bends to loosen them up. They felt great.

He took his notebook out of his backpack and turned to a fresh blank sheet of paper. Carefully he began to copy his list over.

Time to get a fresh start on being cool!

After he finished copying the list, he took

out a red marker and put a big check by 2. GET
JEANS. (AND UNDERWEAR!)

He was proud of that check mark. One
down, two to go. He had actually done one of
his steps! But there were two more left to go
and he was almost out of time.

He had to be cool by tomorrow.

A KISSLESS
MORNING

Robbie woke up early the next morning. No, it hadn't been a dream. There were his new jeans on the foot of his bed.

He jumped out of bed and put them on. They felt soft against his legs—just right. He put on his shirt (with a collar). Even it looked great with jeans.

He pulled out his list and looked at it. The one bright red check mark stood out boldly on the page. "One down," he said to himself with determination. "Two to go!"

He looked at the clock. He had fifteen minutes to convince his mother not to come with him to the bus stop.

Mission Impossible? Nothing is impossible until you try it.

He hurried downstairs.

His father was sitting at the kitchen table reading the newspaper.

"Where's Mom?" Robbie asked.

"She'll be down in a minute," said his father. Robbie sat down at the table. If she was still upstairs, then maybe she wasn't planning to walk him to the bus stop after all.

"She went upstairs to get her jacket."

Yes, she was!

She came down the stairs carrying her jacket. Maybe there was no hope. He looked at the bowl of oatmeal at his place. "Mom," he started without looking up, "I'm in third grade now . . . do you think I could walk up to the bus stop by myself?"

There was a moment of silence. Robbie held his breath.

"Well," his mother began.

"I would watch both ways before crossing the street."

"Well . . ."

"I would look out for cars."

"Okay."

"Not speak to strangers."

"Okay."

"Not go out into the stree . . ."

His mother laughed. "I said 'okay!' You may walk to the bus stop by yourself! After all, you are in third grade now."

She smiled at Robbie's father. That look again! Brother!

He began to eat. He had done it! Two steps were complete!

He finished his breakfast, picked up his backpack, and headed out the door to the bus stop. While he waited for the bus, he pulled out his list and put a big red check beside 3. NO KISSES AT THE BUS STOP. He was almost cool!

As the bus pulled around the corner he caught a glimpse of Bo sitting in his usual seat alone. And he wondered if being cool would save him this time.

A PLAN

"Here," Doug called. He had saved Robbie a seat in the first row. Robbie sat down beside Doug and looked back over his shoulder at Bo.

"What are you going to do?" said Doug. "You can't be Book Buddies with Bo. No one has ever been Book Buddies with Bo before."

"Never?"

"Never. Everyone is afraid of Bo. You'd better tell Ms. Williams you can't do it."

Robbie had never thought of that. He had told his mother that he wanted jeans and she had bought him jeans. He had told his parents not to walk him to the bus stop and had avoided the kisses. Would it be that easy? Could he just tell Ms. Williams that he couldn't be a Book Buddy? Not a bad plan.

"When?" he asked Doug.

"Right before class," said Doug. "Catch her before the bell rings."

Robbie nodded. He hated not to be a Book Buddy but the thought of going out into the hall with Bo was much worse.

The bus pulled up. Robbie hurried into the school. He did not wait for the bell like the other children. He walked straight to his classroom.

"Robbie?" Ms. Williams seemed surprised to see him. "I'm so pleased to have you in my room this year!" She smiled at him.

Robbie smiled back.

This would be easy. He would just say, "I can't be a Book Buddy," and that would be that. He opened his mouth to speak.

"And," she continued, "I'm glad that you will be a Book Buddy this year, especially with Bo Haney."

Robbie closed his mouth and blinked. This was not going the way that he had planned.

"Your last year's teacher and I chose you for a special reason."

"Why?" Robbie asked.

"Well, you are smart and funny and nice."

"I am?"

"You are. And Bo needs someone special to be his Book Buddy. Someone who won't make fun of him. It is always hard for the children who are held back."

"Oh."

Robbie could not say anything for a moment.

How could he ask not to be a Book Buddy now? He even felt a little bit bad for Bo. Asking would not work this time like the jeans and the bus stop. He had to decide for himself.

"We'll start Book Buddies in about fifteen minutes. Did you want to ask me something, Robbie?"

The bell rang and the other kids filed in. He had no time to think about it. He couldn't ask her now. He couldn't avoid Bo now.

"No," said Robbie, "it was nothing."

His plan had not worked. He walked back to his desk and put his head down. In fifteen minutes he would be Book Buddies with Bo.

LAST WILL AND TESTAMENT

Robbie opened his notebook to a blank page and wrote: LAST WILL AND TESTAMENT. That's what people wrote before they died. He looked over at Bo. He didn't have long now. Fifteen minutes at the most.

To my friend, Doug Daniels, I leave my baseball card collection and my throw-yo.

To my neighbor, Tobey, I leave my stuffed animals and my G.I. Joe Action Figures.

To my mother I leave my . . .

"Robbie!" His thoughts were interrupted by Ms. Williams.

"Robbie, it's time for Book Buddies." Ms.

Williams waited at the door with the red folder. Bo was standing beside her. He seemed to fill up the opening of the door. This did not look good.

Robbie got up. He felt the eyes of every student in the class watching him as he walked toward the door.

"Nice knowing you," a voice whispered.

"Good luck, you'll need it," said another voice.

He walked up and stood beside Ms. Williams and Bo. Ms. Williams handed him the red folder. "The first page inside will tell you what to do," she said. "Bo has worked with Ms. Bebee. Bo knows what to do. Don't you, Bo?"

Bo nodded.

Robbie blinked. He could imagine the things that Bo knew how to do. Slow torture. Knuckle sandwich. Indian sunburn.

He took the red folder from Ms. Williams and headed out the door behind Bo. The door slammed shut. Robbie followed Bo down the hall. He watched Bo's shoulders from behind.

Bo had muscles—big muscles. The two desks sat by the wall waiting for them. The hall was dark and empty. It looked bigger than usual with no other kids in it. The hall was quiet— too quiet.

Bo sat down. He filled the small desk like a grown-up. Robbie sat down, too. They looked at each other. He waited for Bo to say something but Bo was silent.

Robbie had to say something now. The right something. His life depended on it. He had seen a cartoon one time where Bugs Bunny lit a fuse to a storehouse full of dynamite. Elmer Fudd had to put out the fuse before it hit the dynamite. Elmer Fudd danced and stomped on the fuse in desperation but it kept on burning. Robbie felt that kind of desperation now. If he could only say the right thing the fuse would go out.

What do you say to a bully? He felt like opening his mouth like Baby Tobey and saying, "*Waaaaa!*" If only he and Bo had one thing in common. One thing to talk about. He looked down at the red folder and saw the name Clyde

Elmer Haney. As much as he hated his own name it wasn't as bad as Clyde Elmer.

"Is this your name?" He pointed to the folder. As soon as he said it he knew that he had said the wrong something. Bo's head snapped around. His eyes looked at Robbie with beady sharpness like a falcon coming in for the kill.

"Yeah!" he snapped. "You want to make something of it?"

Robbie swallowed. "No," he said. "I hate my name, too."

"What's your name?" said Bo. "I mean your real name."

"Robert, Robert Hayes York."

"Huh. That's not bad. You talk about bad—Clyde Elmer. Now that's bad."

Robbie was having a conversation with Bo.

"It's not my real name that I hate," said Robbie. "It's my nickname, Robbie. That's what I hate."

"Yeah," said Bo, nodding. "I would hate that, too. Like Clydie."

Robbie giggled.

"You making fun of me?" The sharpness was back in Bo's eyes.

"No!" said Robbie. "You just said something funny."

"Yeah," said Bo. "Right." Then something amazing happened. The corners of Bo's mouth turned up! Just a little but Robbie was sure that he had seen it. Bo smiled at Robbie.

Sssss! The imaginary fuse went out. The dynamite was not going to blow today.

Bo grabbed the folder and opened it. "You hold up these cards. I say what's on them. If I miss, you tell me."

Robbie pulled the flash cards out of the folder.

He noticed that the hall wasn't completely dark. A ray of light came through the window at the end of the hall and made a small yellow patch on the floor at his feet. He was going to live.

BEING COOL

Robbie heard the door to the classroom open.

He looked down the hall and saw Doug peer around the door. Doug had a green library pass in his hand. Doug had come to check on him.

"Hey, Robbie," Doug called as he walked by the two desks. "Are you . . . okay?"

"Hey!" said Bo. "His name's Rob! And he is fine! Get it? My friend here is fine."

Doug's eyes widened. He didn't stop as he hurried toward the library. "I get it!" Doug said in a small voice on his way down the hall. "I get it!"

"Hey," called Rob as Doug walked away.

"Thanks!" He looked back at Bo and held up another card.

Rob? Bo had changed his name! But not to a name like Squeaky and Al-burp or Wobbie. This time for the better. And when Bo changed a name, it stayed changed!

He had finished his list! He could put a bright red check by each of the three things:

Get rid of the name Robbie. Check—thanks to Bo.

Get jeans. Check. He looked down at his new blue jeans. No one had even noticed them yet.

No kisses at the bus stop. Check. That didn't seem so important now.

So, was he cool now? Yesterday he had thought coolness was an armor against bullies. Maybe it was in a way, but not in the way that he thought. The jeans had not mattered or the kisses or his new name.

He thought about what Ms. Williams had said. Was he smart? He *had* been chosen to be a Book Buddy. Was he funny? Bo seemed to think so. Was he nice? Hadn't he just risked his life to help Bo? He was proud of that. Maybe that's what being cool was all about.

"How about this one, Bo?" He held up another card. They had a lot of work to do. He was too busy to worry about being cool.

It was going to be a great year.

BETSY DUFFEY and **JANET WILSON** have worked on two other popular chapter books together: *The Math Wiz* and *The Gadget War* (both Viking). Ms. Duffey, who also wrote The Pet Patrol books (*Puppy Love*, *Wild Things*, and *Throw-Away Pets*), lives in Atlanta, Georgia, with her husband and two sons. Ms. Wilson and her family live in Toronto, Ontario.